Published by Ladybird Books Ltd
A Penguin Company
Penguin Books Ltd, 80 Strand, London, WC2R 0RL, England
Penguin Books Australia Ltd, Camberwell, Victoria, Australia
Penguin Group (NZ), cnr Airborne and Rosedale Roads, Albany,
Auckland 1310, New Zealand

ISBN-13: 978-1-84646-126-2
ISBN-10: 1-8464-6126-X

Manufactured in Italy

A Day
at the Fair

"Excellent darlinks!" said Miss Lilly at the end of the dance class.

Angelina and her friend, Alice, rushed to get changed.

"Just think, Alice," said Angelina. "In exactly one hour, you and I will be riding on the fastest, scariest rollercoaster in all of Mouseland! Hurry up, William! We'll be late for the fair!"

Angelina rushed home and counted the money in her piggy bank. "Hooray!" she said, "just enough for a candy floss!" Scooping up the coins, she ran to the door.

Unfortunately she bumped straight into Mrs Mouseling and her cousin Henry.

"Excuse me young lady," said her mother. "You promised to look after Henry today." "But I'm going to the fair!" cried Angelina.

"Great!" said Henry. "I love fairs!"

Angelina sighed and, fixing a grin on her face, took him by the hand.

When Angelina and Henry arrived at the
fair, they headed straight for the rides.
"Look at the merry-go-round, Angelina!
I love them. Don't you?" asked Henry.

"No Henry," said Angelina sniffily.
"Merry-go-rounds are for babies."

"And there's a man selling balloons!"
continued Henry. "Can I have a blue
one. Please?"

"No you can't, Henry! I've only got
enough money for a candy floss."
They walked across the noisy fairground
until Angelina found Alice and William.

The four mouselings rushed around the noisy colourful fairground, looking at all the different rides, until at last they came to the big wheel. Henry could hardly see the top of it. It seemed like a very very long way up. Angelina was so excited. She couldn't wait to jump on!

"I told you that I don't really like big wheels," whispered Henry as he squeezed Angelina's hand very tightly.

Angelina bent down to reassure him.
"Don't worry, Henry they're not at all
scary!" she said gently. "Trust me. You're
going to love it!"

Henry reluctantly followed the others and up they went, climbing higher and higher.

"Isn't this fun, Henry!" laughed Angelina.

But poor Henry wasn't having fun at all. In fact he felt quite sick. "I want to get off!" he sobbed loudly.

Angelina was very embarrassed as the huge wheel came to a standstill and an attendant helped Henry step off the ride.

Henry held William's hand as the four
friends queued up for the Haunted House.
But Henry still wasn't happy.

"I told you Angelina. I hate the dark!"

Angelina ignored poor Henry and dragged
him inside. There were spooky noises and
it was almost pitch black! Suddenly,
Henry realised that he was no longer
holding William's hand. He was all alone!

Henry walked bravely through the
darkness, until he thought he saw
William. He reached out his hand.
But, oh no! It was a huge hairy spider.

"Agghhhhh!" screamed Henry.

The lights went on and Henry looked around him. It didn't look so scary any more. He was very pleased to see Angelina and the others just up ahead.

"I'm scared of spiders," sobbed Henry. He felt very shy as the attendant led them all out of the Haunted House. People were watching and Angelina looked very cross. Alice and William wandered off, leaving her with Henry.

"Can I have a blue balloon now?" Henry asked Angelina shyly. "And can I go on the merry-go-round?"

Suddenly, Alice and William rushed up.

"You should have come with us, Angelina.
We've just been on the swinging boat, and
the helter skelter. It was fantastic!"

"It's just not fair," said Angelina crossly.

"You have to come on the Loop the Loop rollercoaster with us. You just HAVE to!" cried Alice.

"I don't like rollercoasters," said Henry. Angelina sighed.

Suddenly, a clown walked by. "Show starts in ten minutes!" he cried. "Wicky wacky fun for all ages!" Angelina smiled. "I bet you like clown shows, don't you Henry?" she said.

At last she was free! She left Henry at
the clown show and soon she, Alice and
William were soaring up high on the
rollercoaster. They loved it so much that
they rode on it SEVEN TIMES!

Henry, meanwhile, wasn't having much fun at the clown show. As his eyes wandered he saw a big blue balloon float past. He just had to go and catch it!

A little while later, Angelina, Alice and William arrived at the clown's tent to collect Henry. But Henry wasn't there.

"Henry?" whispered Angelina. Her heart in her mouth. "Where are you?"

The three friends ran through the crowds calling Henry's name. They looked everywhere. Alice even called up to the stilt walker because he'd be able to see across the whole fairground. But nobody had seen Henry.

At last they sat down on a bench. Alice tried to comfort Angelina and William offered her his hankie to blow her nose. "What am I going to do?" cried Angelina.

Suddenly, Angelina saw a blue balloon
float past, with Henry running along
behind, trying to catch it.
"Henry!" she cried. "Thank goodness!"

Angelina took Henry by the paw and
they set off through the crowds. Angelina
even used her precious coins to buy him
a big blue balloon.
"Look at the merry-go-round Angelina!"
cried Henry. "I love merry-go-rounds."

Angelina smiled as she helped Henry up
onto his favourite ride. "I love merry-go-
rounds, too," she said.